TWISTED
FAIRY TALES

SNOW WHITE AND THE SEVEN ROBOTS

Stewart Ross

ARCTURUS

ARCTURUS

This edition published in 2020 by Arcturus Publishing Limited
26/27 Bickels Yard, 151–153 Bermondsey Street,
London SE1 3HA

Written by: Stewart Ross
Illustrated by: Chris Jevons
Designed by: Jeni Child
Edited by: Sebastian Rydberg

ISBN: 978-1-78950-247-3
CH006828NT
Supplier 13, Date 1119, Print run 9052

Printed in China

Far away, in another galaxy, there lived a powerful queen. Not a nice, smiling queen, but a nasty, mean, and selfish queen.

She was called the Star Queen because she ruled everything—even the stars. But she was unhappy. She spent most of her time looking at pictures of old classmates on Spacebook, her mega computer, and feeling jealous.

One day the Star Queen demanded: "Viewscreen, viewscreen on the wall, who is doing best of all?"

The answer flashed up immediately: "Your daughter, Snow White!"

"Liar!" screamed the Star Queen. "I'm doing best of all. *I've* sent all left-handed people to prison. *I've* used half the water in the galaxy to build an ice palace on a desert planet. And *I* make all the children eat snail porridge every day. Isn't that the best,

Squeezy?" she asked her pet astro-python.

"It is-s-s, O Queen," he hissed.

"And that stupid Snow White has done nothing," she continued. "All she does is fiddle around with machines and wires, and mess about in the vegetable plot. I must get rid of that miserable little girl—NOW!"

At supper that evening, the Star Queen said she needed to visit Prince Cosmos.

"But I'm too busy," she added slyly. "Would you go for me, *dear* Snow White?"

Snow White was good friends with Prince Cosmos. Just like her, he was a keen gardener. "I'll pack some seeds to show him!" she said.

However . . . it was a trap!

The Star Queen had made a special rocket for the trip—it would fly to nowhere and never arrive. Snow White would be stuck in nothingness forever.

"Ha-ha! Serves her right!" cackled the Star Queen as she watched Snow White's rocket take off. "We'll never see *her* again, thank goodness!"

Then she went back to doing what she liked best—building evil robots. Just like her daughter, she was a clever engineer.

In the space rocket, Snow White looked around in horror. *Oh no!* she thought. *Something has gone wrong. We're not going to Prince Cosmos's planet. In fact, we're going . . . nowhere. And very fast!*

Instead of panicking, she rolled up her sleeves and got to work. She did some counting, pressed buttons, joined wires together . . . and slowly, very slowly, she steered the rocket toward a tiny green planet.

Her computer said it was called Planet Smartie.

The rocket still didn't work very well. It wibbled and wobbled before landing with a loud crash!

Snow White picked herself up off the floor and looked out the window. "Hmm, it looks all right," she said to herself. Carefully, she opened the door and stepped outside.

What a strange place! thought Snow White as she walked between weird plants and trees. There were collimunchers with hungry mouths and greedy eyes, and hollygrabbers with branches like arms.

"I'm not sure it's safe," said Snow White to herself. "I think I'd better return to my—eek!"

The twiggy fingers of a hollygrabber had wrapped around her arm. "Let me go— please!" cried Snow White.

It was no good. More twisty twigs coiled about her arms and legs, holding her tight.

The Chief Collimuncher scrabbled up to her. "Sorry about this," it said, "but we're going to eat you."

"Eat me!" she exclaimed. "How horrible! Why me?"

"Because we've got nothing else," explained the collimuncher. "The Star Queen has stolen all our water to build her ice palace, and now the plants we eat won't grow. So all we've got to eat—"

"Wait!" said Snow White, trying to remain calm. "First, I'm not at all tasty—all skin and bones. Second, if you set me free, I'll grow the best food you've ever tasted. Do we have a deal?"

The collimunchers and hollygrabbers chatted together. "Right," said the hollygrabber who had taken ahold of Snow White, "Two weeks—feed us—or else!"

"What my friend means," explained the Chief Collimuncher, "is that if you don't get us food, our next meal will be YOU."

"Fair enough," said Snow White. "A feast for everyone in two weeks. Promise."

"Hmph," sniffed the hollygrabber. "Foolish promise. Just you—food for everyone—impossible!"

Snow White returned to her rocket and brought out a set of tools. "But it won't be just me," she said with a smile. "Watch!"

In four days, using pieces of the broken rocket, she made seven robot helpers.

There was Squeaky, who needed a drop of oil, and Creaky, whose joints weren't quite right. Rusty was made of the oldest rocket pieces, Jerky moved like a puppet, Wonky's head wasn't straight, and Blinky's eyes didn't work too well.

But halfway through the seventh robot, Snow White stopped. Oh dear! She had run out of brain parts.

The seventh robot had a purple plastic body with metal arms and legs. Its square box head had a face with beautiful green eyes and a lovely smile, but inside it was almost empty.

"Sorry, Box," said Snow White sadly, giving him a kiss on his cheek. "I know you're not very smart, but you are *extremely* kind."

"That's all right, Snow White," he said. "Now that I'm finished, may I start work?"

"You sure can!" she cried. "So can the others. Come on, Squeaky, Creaky, Rusty, Jerky, Wonky, and Blinky! Let's get farming!"

In three days, they dug fields and planted some fast-growing seeds that Snow White had packed before leaving.

The collimunchers and hollygrabbers

watched in amazement as the plants grew day and night. After five days, they were ready. Snow White and her robots harvested them and cooked them in huge pots made from leftover pieces of rocket.

That evening the collimunchers and hollygrabbers sat down to the biggest, tastiest meal they'd ever eaten.

Back in her palace, the Star Queen was building her latest invention—deadly robots disguised as delicious fruit! She called them Fruit Fiends. She was frustrated, because she couldn't get the apple to work properly.

"Why don't you just ask Ssspacebook, O Queen?" suggested the astro-python.

"Good idea, for once" said the queen. "But first I'll ask it an important question once more. This time I *know* it'll tell the truth. Viewscreen,

viewscreen on the wall," she cackled, "who is doing best of all?"

Again, the answer flashed up immediately: "Snow White!"

"Impossible!" she screamed. "Show her to me!" The viewscreen played a video of Snow White and her robots enjoying a large meal with the collimunchers and hollygrabbers.

"How horrible!" screeched the queen. "Where are they?"

"On Planet Smartie," replied Spacebook.

"Right," growled the queen. "This time she will not escape!"

She loaded seven Fruit Fiend robots into a Flying Fiend rocket. They looked like a bunch of bananas, an orange, a pear, a bunch of grapes, a pineapple, a melon, and an apple. But they were deadly dangerous.

Guided by Spacebook, the Flying Fiend
rocket zoomed through space to Planet
Smartie. It landed in the field where Snow
White's robots were working.

The door flew open and out rolled the
Fruit Fiend robots, looking like juicy fruits.

"Oh look," said Squeaky, picking up a
banana. "A delicious piece of fruit!"

As he was speaking, the fiend split open
the banana skin and fired a sharp dart

straight at Squeaky's heart. *Ping!* It bounced off his metal body and landed in the mud.

"So that's your nasty trick, is it?" muttered Squeaky. He grabbed the fiend and shoved it into his harvest bag.

Creaky did the same with the fiend inside the orange, Rusty with the pear, Jerky with the bunch of grapes, Wonky with the pineapple, and Blinky with the melon.

But when Box saw the rosy red apple, he thought, *How delicious! A perfect present for Snow White.* He lifted it up carefully and set off to find her.

Box was so set on getting to Snow White that he didn't ask the other robots about their fruits. Instead, he made up a little rhyme and sang it as he walked along:

"I know my brain is not too bright,
But I've got an apple for Snow White.
It's shiny, round, and rosy red,
And it's hers . . ."

He was trying to think of something that rhymed with "red" when he saw Snow White chatting with the Chief Collimuncher.

"Hey, you guys," he called, grinning, "look what I've found!"

"What a beautiful apple!" Snow White said with a smile.

Box blushed and offered it to her. "It's for you," he mumbled.

"Oh, thank you, Box!" said Snow White. She took the apple and turned it around in her hand to find the juiciest part.

This was the moment the sneaky Fruit Fiend had been waiting for. It burst out of the apple and, with a wicked cry, fired its dart straight at Snow White's heart.

When the dart hit her, Snow White gave a little cry.

"What's the matter?" asked Box. "Is it the apple?"

Snow White's eyes began to close. "Not apple," she yawned, "but . . . something . . . inside . . ."

Without another word, she fell to the ground, fast asleep.

Box's green eyes were full of tears as he knelt beside her. "Wake up!" he begged, "Please wake up!"

Snow White did not move.

"A horrid robot-thing was hiding in the apple," the Chief Collimuncher gasped. "Grab it, Box!"

Box seized the Apple Fiend and stuffed it into his bag.

The robots, the collimunchers, and the
hollygrabbers all tried to wake Snow White.
When she remained asleep, they laid her
gently down on a bed of the softest stardust.

Squeaky took Box's bag and shook out
the Apple Fiend. "What did you do?" he
demanded.

"I only fired my dart," it replied, "like
the Star Queen ordered me to. She dipped
the dart in a sleeping potion. When it enters
someone's heart, they fall asleep for a
thousand years."

"A thousand years!" howled Squeaky, Creaky, Rusty, Jerky, Wonky, Blinky, and Box.

"Yes," said the Apple Fiend. "And the only way she will wake up before that is if someone pulls the dart out of her heart."

"I'll do it!" cried Box eagerly. He was keen to make up for his terrible mistake.

"You can't!" sneered the fiend. "The dart is invisible. You can't pull out something you can't see, stupid!"

Squeaky grew even more angry. "All right, you do it, you little monster!" he shouted.

"Why should I, tin-pot?" the fiend replied rudely.

Just as things were becoming a little unpleasant, there was a loud whirring noise. Moments later, a shiny blue spaceship landed on the field. The door opened, and a

handsome young man stepped out.

"Hello, everyone," he said cheerfully. Then, seeing the glum looks on the faces of the robots, he asked, "What's the matter? Are you guys having some sort of problem here? Can I help?"

It was Prince Cosmos.

After Squeaky had explained to the
prince what had happened, he asked if
he could see Snow White. Lying there,
fast asleep, she looked so beautiful.

"There must be a way to wake her,"
he said with a sigh.

"There is," croaked Rusty, "but only the
Apple Fiend can do it."

"Why?"

"Because no one else can see the dart,"
explained Blinky, his eyelashes flapping
like butterfly wings.

This gave Wonky an idea—if the Apple
Fiend took the dart from Snow White's

heart, they would
promise to free all
the Fruit Fiends.

"Great thinking!"
said Prince Cosmos.
But when they
told the Apple Fiend

about it, it shook its spidery head. "No way. First, we can't leave in our rocket because only the Star Queen knows how to start it. Second, we don't *want* to go back to Star Palace. We *hate* the Star Queen. She bullies us and makes us do things we don't want to do—like sending Snow White to sleep!"

Prince Cosmos frowned. "You mean," he said to the Apple Fiend, "none of you actually likes the Star Queen?"

The Apple Fiend nodded. "If we disobey her, she takes out our batteries. And when she's very angry, she pulls off our legs!"

"Ouch! Too cruel." The Prince frowned. "Listen, I have a plan . . ."

But when he explained his idea to the Apple Fiend, it shook its head. "I told you before, our rocket won't work unless the Star Queen starts it."

"Oh yes, it will!" chorused the robots. "Snow White can start it. She can do *anything.*"

"She's the smartest person in the whole universe," added Creaky.

"And the nicest," Box said with a sniff. Prince Cosmos agreed.

"Well, if she's as smart as that," said the Apple Fiend, "I'll see what I can do."

Watching in case it changed its mind and tried to escape, the robots and Prince Cosmos took the Apple Fiend to where Snow White lay on her stardust bed.

Prince Cosmos was biting his fingernails.

Box was crying. "Please wake up, Snow White," he sobbed. "Please! Please!"

The Apple Fiend stretched out two hairy arms, seized something no one else could see—and pulled.

There was a noise like a cork leaving a bottle, and the Apple Fiend fell over backward.

Snow White yawned and slowly opened an eye. Then two eyes. Before long, she was sitting up and talking with her friends.

That afternoon, they held an enormous Smartie party to celebrate her waking up. Now

that everyone knew they weren't really horrible, even the Fruit Fiends were allowed to join in.

When the dancing was over, Snow White set to work on the Flying Fiend rocket. Helped by Squeaky and Rusty, she quickly worked out how to start it.

The Fruit Fiends climbed aboard, and Snow White switched on the engine.

Five, four, three, two, one . . . Liftoff! The rocket was soon out of sight and zooming back toward Star Palace.

The Star Queen was waiting for her
Fruit Fiend robots when they landed.

"What?" she screamed. "Why? And how?
Only I can start that rocket!"

"I will explain," said the Apple Fiend calmly.

"It'd better be good," she snarled.

"The best."

"Best?" she sneered. "My viewscreen tells
me I am *always* doing best of all."

The Apple Fiend shook its head. "I don't

think so. Before we left, I heard it say Snow White was doing best of all."

"Liar!" howled the queen, her silver skin turning red with fury.

"No," replied the Apple Fiend. "Doing best means being kind and helpful, not showing off and bullying people."

The Star Queen had heard enough. She charged at the Fruit Fiends, threatening to remove each of their batteries and use them for spare parts in her washing machine.

"Help, help," squeaked the Fruit Fiends. In a panic, they all fired their invisible darts, piercing her cruel heart. She closed her eyes and slid to the floor. The evil Star Queen would sleep for thousands of years.

Back on Planet Smartie, Snow White and Prince Cosmos were digging and planting more seeds. "But maybe it's time to continue my journey," he said after a few days.

"Where to?" asked Snow White.

"Actually, I'm not sure," he replied. "I came here looking for you . . ."

"And now that you've found me," she said, and smiled, "why don't you stay?"

"May I?"

"Of course!"

He did. And as far as I know, Snow White, Prince Cosmos, the seven robots, the collimunchers, and the hollygrabbers are still there, all very, very happy.